Pony-Crazed Princess

Princess Ellie
to the Rescue

Read all the adventures of Princess Ellie!

Pony-Crazed Princess

Princess Ellie to the Rescue

by Diana Kimpton

Illustrated by Lizzie Finlay

Hyperion Paperbacks for Children
New York

For Jasmine

First published in the United Kingdom in 2004 as
The Pony-Mad Princess: Princess Ellie to the Rescue
by Usborne Publishing Ltd.
Based on an original concept by Anne Finnis
Text copyright © 2004 by Diana Kimpton and Anne Finnis
Illustrations copyright © 2004 by Lizzie Finlay

Printed in the United States of America
First U.S. edition, 2006
3 5 7 9 10 8 6 4 2

This book is set in 14.5 point Nadine Normal.
ISBN# 0-7868-4870-7
Visit hyperionbooksforchildren.com

Chapter 1

"Oh, no," said the princess as the book she'd been balancing on her head crashed to the floor.

Miss Stringle picked it up and sighed as she looked at the title. "Not again, Princess Aurelia. Perhaps you would find waving lessons easier if you practiced more, instead of reading these silly pony stories."

"But I like those silly pony stories. And I

like to be called Princess *Ellie*."

Miss Stringle sighed again. "I've told you before: that is not a suitable name for a princess." She held out the book. "Now, stand as tall as you can, and try once more."

Ellie straightened her head, balanced the book carefully on top of it, and set out across the room. The skirt of her frilly pink dress swirled around her legs as she walked.

"No, no!" shouted Miss Stringle. "Dainty steps. Not big strides."

Ellie slowed down.

"Now wave," said Miss Stringle.

Ellie raised her right hand slowly and waved at an imaginary crowd.

"And smile!"

Ellie pulled her lips back and showed her

teeth. She didn't feel like smiling. She felt very silly. No one in her pony books ever had to do anything like this. They had tons of friends, went to ordinary schools, and spent all their free time having fun with their ponies. All the things that Ellie wanted, but couldn't have. Sometimes Ellie hated being a princess.

She reached the other side of the room

with relief and let the book slide off her head. "I've finished," she said, as she caught it neatly. "May I go now?"

Miss Stringle smiled. "Of course you may, Your Highness. Have a lovely ride."

Ellie raced out of the palace classroom and up the spiral staircase to her bedroom. It was probably the pinkest room in the entire world. Her father, the King, had planned the decorations when she was born; he was convinced princesses liked pink.

Ellie didn't. She had managed to cover the pink walls with lots of pony posters and bookcases full of pony books. But there was nothing she could do about the rose-pink carpet, pink-striped curtains, and pink four-poster bed.

She threw off her dress and grabbed her

pale pink jodhpurs from the closet. As she struggled into them, she glanced at the clock. She didn't want to be late. George always got mad when she was late.

Then she remembered. George wasn't there anymore. After caring for the royal horses for forty years, he had retired. Today she would meet the new groom for the first time.

She pulled on her shiny black leather riding boots, thankful that no one in the kingdom made pink ones her size.

It will be strange to be at the stable without George, she thought. I wonder if the new groom will have as many rules. George had hundreds of them, most of which began, *princesses don't . . .*

Ellie pushed her everyday crown lower on her head and picked up her hard hat. She paused for a moment to straighten its gold-and-pink silk cover. Then she ran out of the room and down the back staircase to the stable.

To her surprise, there was no sign of the new groom. But there was a new horse. A beautiful gray thoroughbred looked out from the stall where George's horse had lived. Ellie walked over to him and stroked his neck. His coat was as soft as velvet. The horse whickered gently and nuzzled her pockets in search of treats.

"Hello."

The cheerful voice made Ellie jump. She turned and saw a tall, slim woman walking toward her carrying a saddle and bridle; she had friendly brown eyes, and her long, dark hair was tied back in a ponytail.

"I see you've met my Gypsy," said the woman as she put the saddle on a saddle rack. "I'm Meg. I'm the new groom. And you, I imagine, are Princess Aurelia."

Ellie nodded nervously.

"That's a real mouthful of a name," continued Meg with a smile. "Are you always called that, or do your friends shorten it?"

"I like to be called Ellie," the princess replied bravely. She didn't mention that she didn't have any real friends or that everyone else insisted on calling her Aurelia or "Your Royal Highness."

"All right, then. Ellie it is." Meg grinned and pulled a sheet of royal notepaper from her pocket. "This note from your father says you want to ride Sundance today."

"Yes, please," said Ellie, hardly able to believe what she'd just heard. Meg was the first person ever to call her Ellie. Maybe everything would be different now. Maybe she could have as much fun with her ponies as the characters did in her pony books.

"Then you'd better get him tacked up. I'll see to Gypsy, and then we can go for a ride."

Meg went into Gypsy's stall, leaving Ellie openmouthed with shock. George had never let her do anything in the stable. Although she had four ponies of her own, she had never been allowed to look after them. She knew "tacking up" meant putting on the saddle and bridle. But she had absolutely no idea how to do it.

Chapter 2

For a moment, Ellie wondered if she should ask for help. But this was the first chance she had ever had to do something in the stable by herself. If Meg realized how little she knew, she might not let her try again.

Tacking up can't be that difficult, she thought. I'm sure I can figure out how to do it.

Ellie walked over to the tack room and hesitated. This had been George's special place. She could almost hear him saying, "princesses don't go in there." But George wasn't around anymore, and Meg had told her to get Sundance's saddle. It must be all right to go in.

Ellie stepped inside and breathed in the smell of leather. The saddles were on racks along one wall, with the bridles hanging underneath. She stared at them nervously.

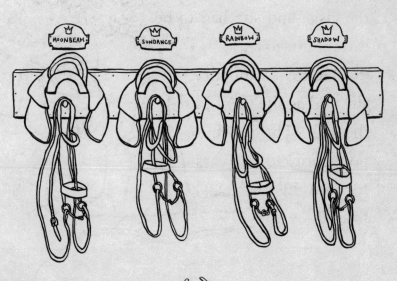

They all looked the same. How could she tell which was Sundance's? Then she realized that above each one was a nameplate, decorated with a golden crown.

Sundance's rack was so high that she had to stand on tiptoe to reach it. The saddle was heavier than she expected. The bridle wasn't, but it was hard to carry them both at the same time. The reins dragged on the ground as she walked down the aisle, and she had to be careful not to trip.

"Hello, Sundance," she said as she went into the stall. The chestnut pony pricked his ears forward in a friendly way and moved toward her. His feet rustled the thick layer of straw on the floor.

"I'm tacking you up today," she told the pony. Her voice sounded more confident than she felt. She carefully put the saddle on the rack, just as Meg had done with Gypsy's. Then she looked at the bridle. She recognized the reins and the metal bit that went in Sundance's mouth. But there seemed to be many other straps and buckles. She wasn't sure which ones she had to undo.

I'll just have to guess, she decided.

She chose one of the buckles and unfastened it. The bit swung down and dangled by one strap. She had no idea if that was supposed to happen. So she picked another buckle and undid that one. The bit fell off completely and landed in the straw. She was sure that that was wrong.

Sundance seemed to think so, too. He put his head down and nuzzled the bit curiously. It didn't help.

Suddenly the door swung open and Meg came in. "How are you doing?" she asked. Then she saw the pieces of the bridle and laughed.

Ellie felt so stupid. This was turning into a terrible day. Nothing was going right; she nearly burst into tears.

But Ellie didn't want Meg to see her cry, so she did the only other thing she could think to do in the situation. She thrust the tangle of straps into Meg's hands, put on her most royal expression, and stormed out of the stall, saying, "princesses don't tack up."

Chapter 3

As soon as Ellie was outside the stall, she felt even more stupid than she had before. She had always wanted to look after her ponies herself, like the characters in her books about ponies. Now she had spoiled the only chance she had ever had to do it.

She sniffed loudly and wiped away a tear with the back of her hand. Then she walked miserably down the aisle to Rainbow's stall.

The gray Welsh pony was standing quietly with her head over the door. Ellie gave Rainbow a mint and stroked her neck. The warm smell of horse made Ellie feel calmer.

She moved along to the next stall and saw Moonbeam, the palomino, quietly eating hay. Moonbeam's mane and tail were snow white, and the rest of her was a beautiful, creamy gold. She came over when she saw Ellie and politely took a mint from her hand.

Then she nuzzled Ellie's pockets looking for more.

Suddenly there was a loud noise from the last stall. Shadow, the black Shetland, had smelled the mints and was banging against the wall to make sure he wasn't forgotten. Ellie ran down the aisle to see him. He was too small to put his head over the door, so she had to reach over and down to give him his treat. She ruffled his mane and sighed as he crunched it. "I've ruined everything," she said.

She heard a clatter of hooves behind her. She turned around and saw Meg leading Sundance.

"I've tacked him up for you," Meg said gently. "Do you still want to ride?"

"Yes, please," said Ellie, her voice unsteady

as she fought back tears. "And I'm sorry I was rude to you before."

"That's all right," said Meg. "It was wrong of me to laugh. I should have checked to see that you knew what to do." She pulled down the stirrups and held Sundance's reins. "Now, jump on, and we'll have a nice ride to cheer you up."

Ellie felt better once she was on Sundance's back. She leaned forward and patted the chestnut pony's neck while she watched Meg mount Gypsy. Then she followed her out of the stable area and onto the palace grounds.

They rode side by side. "Did you mean what you said in the stable?" Meg asked. "You don't have to tack up if you don't want to."

"But I do," said Ellie quickly. "I want to tack up and groom and clean out the stalls and feed the ponies and clean the saddles and everything." Then she stopped and added

quietly, "But I don't know how. George never let me."

"Then I'd better teach you," said Meg. "But before I do that, let's gallop across this field. Unless princesses *don't* gallop."

Ellie laughed happily. "This one does," she said.

"Follow me then," said Meg, and she raced away on Gypsy.

Ellie squeezed her legs against Sundance's sides. The pony took off willingly and galloped after the gray thoroughbred. Ellie leaned forward in the saddle and felt the wind whistle past her face. She could hear Sundance's hooves drumming on the ground as the pony carried her swiftly across the grass.

As they neared the other side of the field,

Sundance started to tire. Ellie let him slow to a gentle canter until they reached the fence where Meg was waiting. Then they rode slowly along the edge of the field, letting Sundance and Gypsy catch their breath.

A fox trotted across their path. It stopped for a moment to look at them before continuing calmly on its way. Ellie watched as it squeezed under the fence and disappeared into a patch of woodland. She peered between the trees, trying to catch another glimpse of it. But instead of the fox, she saw a human face looking back at her.

Suddenly a bird flew out from the bushes and startled Sundance. He snorted with fear and jumped sideways. The movement took Ellie by surprise. Her left foot came out of its stirrup, and for a moment she thought she was going to fall off. But she managed to stay in the saddle and quickly calmed her pony down.

"Good save," said Meg as Sundance walked forward again.

Ellie glowed with pride. Then she looked back at the woods. The face had gone. Perhaps she had imagined it. But as they rode away, she had the strangest feeling that she was being watched.

Chapter 4

The pleasure of riding soon stopped Ellie from wondering any more about the mysterious watcher. By the time they got back to the royal stable, she had forgotten the whole incident. "That's the best ride I've ever had," she told Meg. "I loved that gallop."

"So did I," said Meg. "Now, put Sundance in his stall and I'll show you how to look after him."

First, Meg taught Ellie how to run the stirrups up to the top of the saddle and undo the girth so the saddle came off easily. Then she showed her which strap to undo on the bridle and how to pull it off gently so that the bit fell out of Sundance's mouth without banging against his teeth. Finally, Meg handed Ellie a brush and told her to brush the saddle mark off the pony's back, while she went to put the saddle and bridle away.

Ellie was very happy. It was warm in the stable, and it smelled of horse. For the first time, Sundance really felt like Ellie's own pony.

"Is there anything else I can do?" she asked when Meg came back.

"You can help me give the ponies their hay and fill the water buckets if you like. But don't you have to get back for dinner?"

Ellie knew it was getting late, but she was reluctant to leave when she was enjoying herself so much. "I've got tons of time," she said, knowing it wasn't really true. It wouldn't matter, she thought, if she was late just this once.

Meg took her to the hayloft and showed her how to fill the stalls with armfuls of soft, sweet-smelling hay. "Make sure it's hay, not

straw," she said. "It's easy to tell the difference. The straw has thicker stems."

The job took much longer than Ellie had
expected, and it was nearly dark by the time
they had finished. Meg went to check on
Gypsy while Ellie filled the water buckets.
She had never carried buckets full of water

before and was surprised by
how heavy they were. To
make matters worse,
the water slopped
all over as she
walked, so her
jodhpurs and boots
were soon soaked.

"You really need some muck boots," said
Meg when she saw how wet Ellie was. "And
it might be a good idea to leave your crown
at home."

"It's only my everyday one," said Ellie.
"Mom and Dad would be mad if I didn't
wear it. But they might agree to boots. I'll ask
them this evening." Then she remembered.

That evening the prime minister was coming to dinner. It was really important that she get there on time. She'd be in real trouble if she were late. She glanced at her watch in panic. "Oh, no!" she cried. "I'm late. I've got to go." She dumped the last bucket into Sundance's stall and shut the door. Then she ran out of the stable.

"Thanks for your help," Meg shouted after her. "See you in the morning."

Ellie paused just long enough to wave good-bye before running to the back door of the palace and racing up the stairs to her bedroom.

The clock beside her bed stared at her accusingly. Its bright pink hands showed that she had only five minutes to get clean, changed, and make it down to the dining room.

Ellie glanced at herself in the long mirror on the wall. She didn't look much like a princess at the moment. Her face was dirty, her hair was a mess, and her cheeks were red from excitement and exercise.

There's no time for a shower, she thought as she pulled off her jacket and shirt. I'll just have to do the best I can.

She washed her hands quickly, wiped the dirt off her face with a wet towel, and pulled the hay out of her curly blond hair with a comb. Then she popped her tiara on to her head and slipped on one of her best dresses. It was a deep rose pink with sequins on the bodice and several layers of mesh petticoat under the knee-length skirt. Ellie's fingers struggled with the white satin sash as she tried to tie it in a bow behind her back.

As soon as she had succeeded, she ran down the spiral staircase and along the corridor to the dining room. Her feet were almost silent on the thick red carpet. She paused outside the door, smoothing the folds of her skirt as she tried to calm herself. Then she stood up straight, as Miss Stringle had taught her to do, and went in.

The King and Queen were already at the table chatting to the prime minister. They all looked up when she arrived. The King and Queen smiled proudly when they saw Ellie. But slowly their smiles changed to frowns of surprise. They seemed to be staring directly at her feet.

Ellie looked down and groaned. Sticking out from under the bottom of her dress were a pair of very dirty jodhpurs and an even dirtier pair of boots. She had been in such a rush that she'd forgotten to take them off.

Chapter 5

Ellie wondered desperately what to do. Should she leave or should she stay? Then she made up her mind. She couldn't keep them waiting even longer while she changed. She'd just have to act as though nothing were wrong.

Trying to look more confident than she felt, she strode over to the candlelit table and calmly sat down in her place. "I'm so sorry to have kept you waiting," she said.

To her relief, the Queen followed Ellie's lead. "Well, at least you're here now," she said, waving to the servants to bring in the food.

Ellie was determined not to do anything else wrong. She tried hard to eat her meal in the way Miss Stringle had taught her. She chose the correct knife and fork from the gleaming selection by her plate, kept her mouth closed while she chewed, and only spilled a couple of drops of gravy on the crisp, white tablecloth. She even remembered not to drum her feet against the chair leg or play with her crystal glass while the adults talked politics.

At first, the smell of wet jodhpurs and horse was hardly noticeable. But the room was very warm, and the warmth made the smell grow stronger and stronger. By the time they had finished their strawberries and ice cream, Ellie was sure it was impossible to ignore.

She looked nervously around the table to see if any of the others had noticed. The prime minister obviously had. When he realized she was looking at him, he wrinkled his nose and sniffed dramatically.

"How are things down at the stable?" he asked with a smile.

"They're wonderful," said Ellie. "We have a new groom, and she's going to let me look after my ponies myself."

"Really!" said the Queen with surprise. "And what exactly does that involve?"

"It's grooming and cleaning out stalls and cleaning tack and filling buckets and . . ."

"But that's work," said the King. "You're a princess, Aurelia, and princesses don't work."

Ellie stared at him in dismay. What if he wouldn't allow her to look after her ponies? What if he sent Meg away and got another groom like George? "But it's much more fun than sitting in the palace alone," she said.

"That doesn't make any difference," said the King firmly.

The prime minister coughed gently, to

catch their attention. "Perhaps it is more a hobby than work," he said, winking at Ellie.

Ellie grinned back at him in delight. "That's right," she said bravely. "It's definitely a hobby. And I'm sure princesses are allowed to have hobbies."

definitely
for sure

The Queen smiled. "I'm sure they are, too," she said, "provided they remember to get changed before they come to dinner."

Ellie was so happy that she jumped up and kissed her mom. "I promise I will," she said. Then she gave a small curtsy and left the room.

She decided not to mention the muck boots. It seemed more sensible to quit while she was ahead.

Chapter 6

The next morning, Ellie leaped out of bed as soon as she woke up. It was Saturday, so there was no schoolwork. Instead, she could spend the whole day at the stable.

She was already dressed by the time the maid arrived with her breakfast on a silver tray. Ellie ignored the boiled egg, but gulped down the orange juice.

Then she grabbed the buttered toast and ate it as she ran down to the stable.

"I thought you and Sundance might like a lesson today," said Meg. "But first we'll need to turn the other ponies out into the field."

Ellie chose to lead Shadow. She thought he would be the easiest, because he was the smallest. She was wrong. Rainbow and Moonbeam walked quietly, but Shadow didn't want to. Every few steps he dropped his head to grab a mouthful of grass, or dived into the trees to eat some tasty leaves. Soon, Ellie's arm ached from being yanked in one direction after another.

She was relieved when they reached the field. Meg turned Rainbow and Moonbeam loose first. They trotted across the grass together, arching their necks and sniffing the

morning air. Ellie watched them go. Then
she carefully unbuckled Shadow's halter and
took it off. But the little Shetland did not
seem interested in running around. He didn't
go anywhere. He just started eating the grass
right in front of him.

Back at the stable, Meg helped Ellie groom
Sundance. He seemed to enjoy it and lifted his
feet willingly so that
Ellie could clean them
out with a hoof pick.
When Sundance's coat
was gleaming and his
hooves were freshly
coated with oil, Meg
showed Ellie how to put
on his saddle and bridle.
Then they set off for the

riding ring to have a lesson. It was a big area of sand with a wooden fence around the outside and some jumps in the middle.

Ellie had ridden there many times with George, but this time she felt very nervous. She was worried Meg would think that her riding wasn't good enough. She tried hard to keep her heels down and her back straight as she trotted Sundance around the ring. The pony wasn't worried at all. He trotted confidently, with his head up and his ears pricked forward. Soon, Ellie relaxed, too, and started to enjoy herself. Meg was a good teacher and quick to praise everything she did right.

"Now let's see how well you ride without stirrups," said Meg.

Ellie was horrified. No one had ever asked her to do that kind of riding before.

"I can't," she said. "I'll fall off."

"No, you won't," said Meg. She helped Ellie cross her stirrups over the front of the saddle so they were out of the way. "Now, off you go. It's not as hard as you think."

Ellie was scared, but she squeezed with her legs and Sundance walked forward. Maybe Meg was right. It felt strange riding without stirrups, but it wasn't difficult.

"Now trot on," called Meg.

Trotting was much harder. Ellie bumped and bounced so much in the saddle that she had to grab Sundance's mane to steady herself. As they went around the first corner, she slipped sideways and thought she was going to slide right off. Sundance stopped before she had a chance to fall.

"He's worried about you," said Meg.

"He's stopping because he doesn't think you're safe."

"I don't think I am, either," said Ellie, as she gave the chestnut pony a grateful pat.

"You're leaning forward. That's what's causing the problem. You'll find it much easier if you sit up straight."

Ellie felt more confident knowing that Sundance was trying to help. As he started to trot again, she tried hard to keep her head up and her shoulders back. It made a big difference. She didn't bounce nearly as much, and she felt much safer. Ellie felt as if she were really getting the hang of

44

it. Riding without stirrups wasn't so bad!

Suddenly, she spotted a flash of green beside the stable. There was someone there. She turned her head to see better. But she accidentally leaned forward at the same time and started to bump around again. Ellie had to stop looking in order to get her balance back. She just had enough time to see a girl peering out from behind the stable—a girl who was watching her.

Ellie was sure the girl's face was the one she'd seen the day before. But she didn't have another chance to look until Sundance trotted back past that part of the ring again. By then, the watcher had gone.

Chapter 7

Ellie kept a lookout for the mystery stranger as she rode back to the stable. But she didn't see anyone.

I hope that girl's gone for good, she thought. I don't like her watching me.

She untacked Sundance without any help and brushed away the mark left by the saddle. Then she led him out to the field and turned him loose with the others.

Sundance bucked playfully as he trotted away. Then he rolled on the grass to give his back a good scratch. When he had finished, he stood up and shook himself from nose to tail before finally settling down to graze.

"Now it's time to clean out the stalls," said Meg. She gave Ellie a wheelbarrow, a pitchfork, a shovel, and a broom, and showed her how to take the manure and dirty straw out of Sundance's stall.

It was a completely new experience for Ellie. She had never done such a dirty job before, and at first, the smell of the straw made her wrinkle her nose. Soon she got used to it, however, and worked her way slowly and carefully through the stalls. When she had filled all of them with clean bedding, she swept the floor so that everything looked neat and tidy. Then, feeling very pleased with herself, she set off to the muck heap, her wheelbarrow piled high with wet, dirty straw.

When she arrived, she realized she had to push it right to the top before she could empty it. There were some planks of wood for the wheelbarrow, but it was still hard to make it go up such a steep slope. Her first attempt failed. The wheelbarrow just stopped

halfway up and then rolled down again,
pulling her with it.

Maybe I need more speed, she thought.

She pulled the wheelbarrow back far
enough to get a running start. Then she
raced toward the heap as fast as she could.

The wheelbarrow shot up the planks,
bouncing slightly as it went. Ellie kept

pushing hard until suddenly the wheelbarrow dropped off the end of the last plank. The wheel sank into the soft straw, and the wheelbarrow stopped. Ellie, however, couldn't. She bumped into the wheelbarrow, which promptly tipped over sideways. She went with it, fell over the handle, and landed flat on her face in the dirty straw.

Luckily, the heap of straw was soft, so only her pride was hurt.

Thank goodness no one saw me, she thought as she struggled to her feet.

But then she heard a sound. It was muffled, and it stopped almost as soon as it had started, but she was sure it was a laugh.

Ellie looked around. Meg was still in the yard, but the noise had come from the stable. There was someone in there, watching her. It must be that girl again! This time Ellie wasn't going to let her get away.

She ran toward the source of the sound, slipping and sliding as she came down the giant pile. As she raced through the door of the stable, she caught a brief glimpse of two legs disappearing through a window.

By the time she reached the window and looked out, there was no one to be seen. The watcher had disappeared again, but this time she'd left something behind. It was a piece of green cloth, caught on a nail that stuck out of the wood.

Ellie pulled it off and looked at it. Whoever had been watching her had been wearing a green fleece. And now they were wearing a fleece with a hole in it.

Ellie wondered if she should tell anyone what she'd seen. But she decided not to. It was only a girl—a girl who had no right to be there.

This is my stable, and these are my ponies, thought Ellie. I can handle this myself.

She put the piece of material into the pocket of her jodhpurs and went back to help Meg.

Chapter 8

That night the weather changed. High winds brought dark clouds rolling in from the west, and heavy rain lashed at the palace windows. In the morning, the noise of the storm made Ellie wake up earlier than usual. She lay in bed wishing she could spend all day at the stable again. But she couldn't. She had to go with her parents to visit her great-aunt Edwina, who lived in a completely boring house with no animals, no games, and no TV, out in the country.

Ellie knew she could ride when she got back, but that seemed like such a long time away. She wanted to see her ponies before that. So she got out of bed, slipped into her riding clothes, and crept downstairs.

She opened the side door quietly, pulled up the hood of her raincoat, and ran across to the stable. Gypsy put his head over the door of his stall when he heard Ellie's footsteps. He looked as if he had only just woken up. There were strands of straw caught in his mane from where he'd been lying down.

Ellie stroked the gray horse and looked across at the other ponies' stalls. It was only then that she realized something was wrong. Sundance's door was wide open.

She raced across the rain-soaked yard and looked inside. But she was too late. The stall was empty. Sundance had disappeared.

For a moment, Ellie was so shocked that she couldn't think what to do. Then she rushed back to the palace, calling for help.

Her shouts echoed through the building. Doors flew open in response, and soon she was surrounded by maids, cooks, and the butler, all asking what was wrong.

"Out of my way," shouted the King, as he pushed his way through the crowd. When he reached Ellie, he knelt down and hugged her. "What on earth's happened?" he asked gently.

"It's Sundance," sobbed Ellie. "He's gone."

"Call security! Call out the guards!" shouted the Queen, who had just rushed up in her red velvet dressing gown and silk pajamas. Her everyday crown was perched on top of her curlers.

Ellie led her parents down to the stable to show them the empty stall. The butler came with them, carrying a huge umbrella to protect everyone from the pouring rain.

Meg was waiting for them. She looked as upset as Ellie felt. "I checked on the ponies just before I went to bed," she said. "Sundance was definitely there then."

"He must have been stolen," said the Queen. "Whoever could have done such a dreadful thing?"

The King looked around carefully, as if he were searching for clues. "It looks as if whoever it was knew where Sundance would be." He paused and rubbed his chin thoughtfully. "That's strange," he went on in a puzzled voice. "It must be someone who's been to the stable before."

His words sent a shiver down Ellie's spine as she remembered the mysterious stranger.

"There's been a girl hanging around," she said. "I've seen her watching me and Sundance."

Everyone stared at her in horror.

"Aurelia!" cried the King. "You should have told us."

Ellie burst into tears. "I wish I had," she sobbed. "I'm really sorry. I thought I could handle it. I never dreamed she'd do anything awful like this." She sniffed loudly and wiped away the tears with her hand in a most unprincesslike fashion.

The Queen swiftly passed her a white lace-trimmed handkerchief. "Well, at least you've told us now," she said calmly.

Suddenly there was a commotion on the other side of the stable. A soldier came in leading a girl by the arm. "I found her outside," he said. "She insists she wants to talk to the princess."

The girl was about Ellie's age. She was soaking wet, and her long, straight hair was matted. The zipper on her worn jacket was undone; underneath it she was wearing a green fleece—a fleece with a hole of a very familiar shape.

"She's the thief!" yelled Ellie. She pulled the

piece of green material from her pocket and held it up to show that it was a perfect match.

"I'm not!" shouted the girl as she pulled her arm free of the soldier's grasp. "I'm Kate. I'm staying with my grandparents. My grandmother's the palace cook."

Ellie stared at her suspiciously. "So why were you watching me?" she asked.

For the first time, Kate looked slightly guilty. "Grandma told me not to bother you," she said. "But I love horses so much I just wanted to be near them."

The Queen stepped forward and pointed at her accusingly. "Is that why you stole Princess Aurelia's pony?" she asked.

"I didn't take him," said Kate. "No one did. He got out by himself."

"Nonsense," said the King. "Horses can't open doors."

"Some of them can," said Meg thoughtfully. She closed the stall door and tested the bolt. It slid backward and forward easily. "Maybe Sundance just learned."

Kate rushed over and grabbed Ellie by the hands. "You've got to believe me," she pleaded. "I came to see the ponies really early, before anyone was up. I saw Sundance undo the bolt with his tongue and run off, so I followed him. I thought I could catch him and bring him back. But he's fallen in a ditch, and now he can't get out."

Ellie felt her stomach knot with fear. She couldn't bear it if anything happened to Sundance. "What are we going to do?" she asked. "We've got to save him."

"We'll send out a rescue team," said her father. He listened carefully as Kate described the exact position of the ditch. Then he shook his head. "It'll take a long time to get heavy-lifting gear out there."

Ellie imagined how frightened Sundance must have been. "We can't leave him on his own," she said. "I'll run ahead and keep him calm."

"But princesses don't . . ." began her father, stepping in front of her to block her path.

"This one does," said Ellie, as she ducked past him and ran off into the pouring rain.

Kate ran after her. "You'll get there quicker if I show you the way."

Behind them, Ellie could hear voices shouting, "Come back," and, "Be careful," but she didn't care. All that mattered was making sure Sundance was safe.

Chapter 9

Ellie and Kate ran side by side up the path and across the field to a stream; normally this was a gentle, babbling brook, but the rain had swollen it into a torrent. As their feet pounded across the wooden bridge, Ellie glanced over the side at the deep, fast-flowing water. She felt a shiver of fear. The rain would be filling the ditch as well.

"This way," said Kate when they reached

the other side. She led Ellie up a slope and then turned right, into the woods.

To Ellie's relief, the trees gave them a little shelter from the wind and rain. She was already soaking wet, and she was tired, too. Running so far and so fast was hard work, and she wasn't used to it. But she couldn't stop now. Sundance needed her.

They ran through the woods, twisting and turning between the trees until they came to a large area of sloping ground.

"Sundance is down there," said Kate.

It was difficult to run down the hill. The girls' feet slipped and slithered on the wet grass. But they didn't stop until they reached the ditch where Sundance was trapped. It was deeper than Ellie had expected. Its sides were steep and muddy. Large grooves showed where Sundance's hooves had slid in the mud as he had tried unsuccessfully to climb out.

Ellie's eyes filled with tears when she saw the chestnut pony. He was completely exhausted by his efforts to escape, and was lying on his side in the shallow water at the bottom of the ditch. Luckily, his head was resting a little way up the bank, just clear of the surface of the water, so he could still breathe.

"Sundance! Sundance!" Ellie called.

"We're here, and there's help on the way."

The pony lifted his head slightly when he heard her voice, and whickered gently. Then his head fell back on to the bank and he lay still.

"He's too tired and weak to save himself," said Ellie. "He can't even stand up."

Kate nodded. "That's not the only problem. There's much more water in the ditch than when I left."

"And it's still raining," said Ellie with alarm. "If the water keeps rising, his head will be under the water, and he'll drown."

"I hope the rescue party gets here soon," said Kate nervously.

"So do I," said Ellie. "But we can't let him die. It's up to us to keep him safe until they arrive."

They skidded down the bank to where Sundance lay. Ellie gently stroked his nose, and the pony flicked his ears slightly in response. "He's so cold and wet," she said. "We've got to do something to warm him up."

She took off her jacket and laid it over the part of his body that was still clear of the water. Kate put hers over him, too. They both shivered as the rain soaked quickly through their fleeces.

"If we're colder, he must be warmer," said Kate.

Ellie had another idea. "I read in one of my pony books that a horse feels warmer if his ears are warm," she said. So they crouched down and rubbed Sundance's cold, wet ears, trying to warm them in their hands.

The rain continued to pour down, and the water in the ditch rose higher and higher. Soon it lapped at Sundance's nose. The pony made a feeble effort to lift it clear. Then his head dropped back.

Ellie sat down in the mud and lifted Sundance's head on to her lap. Her legs were in the water now. It was freezing cold, but at least Sundance was safe for a little longer.

Kate sat down beside her. "Let's talk," she said as they huddled together for warmth.

"It'll take our minds off how cold and wet we are."

Ellie stroked Sundance's head and concentrated on Kate's voice as she described how her dad's job took him and her mom all over the world. She'd gone with them when she was younger. Now that she was older, she was staying with her grandparents so she didn't have to keep changing schools.

When Kate stopped talking, Ellie's mind immediately snapped back to the present. She realized with a shudder that the water had risen even higher. She didn't want to think what would happen if the others didn't get here soon. "Let's keep talking," she said. "It's my turn now."

She had just started describing a lesson in royal waving when she heard a shout. She looked over her shoulder and saw Meg, her father, and several other people waving wildly at them. The rescue party had arrived. But were they in time to save Sundance?

Chapter 10

Meg slithered down the bank toward them. She was holding a wide canvas strap with a ring at each end. "We've got to put this around Sundance's belly so we can pull him free."

Ellie held Sundance's head safely on her lap while Meg and Kate waded into the water, struggling to get the strap into position. It would have been impossible if he'd been lying on hard ground. But the mud that had trapped the pony was just soft enough to let them slowly wiggle the strap underneath him.

As soon as it was in place, the men up on the bank let down a long rope with a hook on the end. Meg grabbed it and clipped it onto the rings. "We're ready," she shouted.

Ellie heard the roar of a tractor's engine and saw the rope pull tight. The strap around Sundance tightened, too. The pony felt it and started to panic. Summoning the last of his energy, he started to thrash his legs wildly to escape the strap.

Ellie stroked his head. "Steady, boy," she said. "Stay still. It'll all be over soon."

Sundance flicked his ears toward her voice and grew calmer.

"Keep going," said Meg. "He likes the sound of your voice."

So Ellie kept talking. She told him how beautiful he was and how much she loved him. She talked about the warm stall waiting for him and the wonderful rides they would have together. Sundance listened to her and lay still while the tractor pulled him slowly up the bank to safety.

As soon as he was out of the ditch, everyone rushed to help him. Meg started to rub him dry with towels. The tractor driver put some blankets over him, and the vet listened to his heart with a stethoscope.

Ellie and Kate watched anxiously as they stood shivering in the rain. At last, the vet straightened up and smiled at them. "He's going to be fine," he said. "He just needs to

get warm and have a good, long rest."

The two girls sighed with relief. Then Ellie grabbed some towels and went to help Meg. But the King took hold of her arm and stopped her.

"You've done enough already," he said. He looked at both Kate and Ellie. "You were naughty to run off like that, but you saved Sundance's life. Now you both need to get dry and warm yourselves."

"But I can't leave him now," said Ellie through chattering teeth.

"Your mother guessed that," he said with a laugh. "That's why she's put dry clothes and towels in the back of the car." He turned to Kate and added, "There's some for you, too. And your grandmother insisted on packing hot chocolate and cookies."

It felt wonderful to climb into the car, away from the wind and rain. Ellie and Kate peeled off their wet clothes and wrapped themselves in thick, fleecy towels. They rubbed their arms and legs hard to bring back some warmth into them, and as soon as they were dry, they put on their clean clothes.

Kate found the hot chocolate and poured

out two cups. The girls sat together warming their hands on the hot mugs while they watched the rescuers helping Sundance. He was starting to move now. He lifted his head to look around. Then, with a huge effort, he heaved himself to his feet.

The girls joined in the cheers and watched Meg lead him into the trailer behind the car. Then they ate the cookies, to celebrate, as they drove back to the stable.

When they arrived, Meg lowered the ramp on the trailer, but she didn't go in.

"You lead him out," she said to Ellie. "He's your pony."

Ellie went into the trailer and untied Sundance. As she led him to the top of the ramp, she saw Kate looking at her. Ellie paused for a moment as memories of the last few days raced through her brain—the face in the woods, running through the rain, and huddling together in the ditch with Sundance and Kate. Then she made up her mind and took a deep breath. "I don't want you watching me anymore," she said.

Kate looked embarrassed and stared at her feet. "I won't," she muttered. "I promise." She turned to go.

"Don't be silly," said Ellie. She smiled at Kate. "I don't want you watching me, because I want you to *ride* with me."

Kate turned back quickly. Her face lit up with a huge smile. "That would be great!" she said.

"Come and help, then," said Ellie, with a laugh.

Together, they led Sundance down the ramp and into his stall. Princess Ellie felt blissfully happy. At last, she had a friend to share her ponies with.

Here's a sneak peek at the next adventure
of the

Pony-Crazed Princess

in

Princess Ellie's Secret

Princess Ellie's Secret

Chapter 1

"Steady, Shadow," said Princess Ellie. The black Shetland pony she was riding pawed at the ground with his tiny front hoof. He was eager to start the relay race and couldn't understand the delay.

"Are you all right all the way down there?" asked Kate, with a grin. She was riding Sundance, Ellie's chestnut pony, who was much taller than Shadow.

Ellie grinned back. "Just you wait," she said. "Sometimes it's good to be small." She was so glad Kate had come to live with her grandparents, who worked at the palace. It was good to have a friend at last, and they had a lot of fun together with Ellie's four ponies.

"Are you two ready?" called Meg, the palace groom. When they both nodded, she shouted, "One, two, three, go."

The two ponies leaped forward and galloped across the field toward two piles of clothes on the other side. Ellie leaned forward, urging Shadow on. But the Shetland, with his short legs, was no match for Sundance. The chestnut pony pulled ahead; he reached Kate's pile of clothes first.

Oh, no, thought Ellie, as she saw Kate

leap off Sundance and start putting on a long, floppy coat.

Shadow finally reached the other pile, and Ellie had to concentrate on her own part in the race.

Jumping off Shadow was easy—Ellie's feet were nearly touching the ground anyway. Then she pulled on a long coat, wrapped a scarf around her neck, and crammed a wide-brimmed hat on top of her pink-and-gold riding helmet.

She glanced over at Kate, expecting to see her making her way back. But she wasn't. She was struggling to mount Sundance. Now that she was dressed up it was hard for her to lift her foot high enough to reach the stirrup.

"We've still got a chance, Shadow," cried

Ellie. She didn't have Kate's problem. Shadow was so small that she was able to jump into the saddle without even using the stirrups.

She urged the Shetland into a gallop and headed back toward the finish line. Soon she could hear Sundance's hooves pounding after them, but this time the lead was too great. Shadow raced across the line just ahead of the chestnut pony.

"Ellie's the winner," shouted Meg.

"Well done," said Kate. "Being small was definitely an advantage that time."

Suddenly a voice called out, "Princess Aurelia!"

Ellie looked around and saw Miss Stringle standing at the end of the field near the palace. Miss Stringle always insisted on using Ellie's full name. To Ellie's annoyance, so did nearly everyone else in the royal household, especially the King and Queen. Ellie trotted Shadow across the field to say hello. But as soon as she was close enough to see her governess's face, she realized something was wrong.

"Whatever are you doing, Your Royal Highness?" asked Miss Stringle, giving Ellie one of her disapproving looks.

Ellie ignored the look and cheerfully replied, "We're playing mounted games. You know, when we use the ponies to help. I just won. Did you see?"

"Indeed I did," declared Miss Stringle. "And I'm horrified to see you making such an exhibition of yourself. It is not suitable behavior for a princess."

Ellie felt confused. What, she wondered,

was wrong with winning a race? Then she remembered the hat, coat, and scarf. "I had to wear these," she explained, as she pulled off the hat. "You can't be in this type of relay race without dressing up."

"I am not talking about the clothes," said Miss Stringle. "It's the pony that's the problem. It's much too small." As she spoke, she waved her hand at Shadow. The greedy Shetland instantly assumed he was being offered food. He stuck out his nose and nuzzled Miss Stringle's outstretched palm. She pulled her hand away quickly and dabbed it clean with a lace-trimmed hankie.

Normally, Ellie would have been tempted to laugh. But this time, she was too angry. "Shadow's not too small," she said. "He's exactly the right size for a Shetland."

"But that's not the right size for *you*," said Miss Stringle. "You look ridiculous. I'll have to tell your parents." Without waiting for Ellie to reply, she marched back to the palace with a determined look on her face.

Ellie's heart sank. Deep down inside, she knew Miss Stringle was right.

Shadow was her very first pony, and she could hardly remember a time when he hadn't been there for her to love. He'd been her best birthday present the year she was four, and he'd been just the right size for her then. But over the years, she had grown, and he hadn't. Now her feet nearly touched the ground when she was riding him. She had hoped no one else would notice. But now someone had. What would happen to Shadow if she couldn't ride him anymore?

To find out what happens next, read

Princess Ellie's Secret